Why Cowboys Sleep with Their Boots On

Why Cowboys Sleep

By Laurie Lazzaro Knowlton
Illustrated by James Rice

with Their Boots On

PELICAN PUBLISHING COMPANY
Gretna 1997

*To my Creator
and all those who believed in me—
thank you*

*The word "Pelican" and the depiction of a pelican are trademarks
of Pelican Publishing Company, Inc.,
and are registered in the U.S. Patent and Trademark Office.*

Library of Congress Cataloging-in-Publication Data

Knowlton, Laurie Lazzaro.
    Why cowboys sleep with their boots on / by Laurie Lazzaro Knowlton
; illustrated by James Rice.
        p. cm.
    Summary: A hardworking cowboy who wears his clothes to bed sleeps
so soundly he isn't aware how, during each night, he is losing an
item of clothing.
    ISBN 1-56554-094-8
    [1. Cowboys—Fiction. 2. Desert animals—Fiction.] I. Rice,
James, 1934- ill. II. Title.
PZ7.K7685Wh 1995
[Fic]—dc20   94-24803
                                                            CIP
                                                            AC

Printed in Hong Kong

Published by Pelican Publishing Company, Inc.
1101 Monroe Street, Gretna, Louisiana 70053

Why Cowboys Sleep with Their Boots On

Slim Jim Watkins was one tired cowboy. Sliding out of his saddle, Slim Jim Watkins popped the dirt from his britches. Seemed like he'd lassoed and branded more than a thousand Longhorn. All of this didn't mind him much. He just wanted to go to bed.

So Slim Jim Watkins stripped off his clothes, all but his long johns, and crawled into his bedroll. No sooner did he lay his head on his cowboy hat than Slim Jim Watkins was sound asleep.

"Rise and shine!" bellowed the chuck-wagon cook.

Slim Jim Watkins stretched, groaned, and reached for his britches.

"My britches! They're gone!"

Slim Jim Watkins searched and searched, but he couldn't find his britches.

"This is enough to sour a man's outlook for the day."

Grumbling, Slim Jim Watkins slipped his chaps over his long johns and went to work.

"Dern!" griped Slim Jim Watkins. "These long johns are wearin' thin. I need my britches!"

So after a long day's work, Slim Jim Watkins went to town to buy new denim britches.

It was dark when Slim Jim Watkins rode back to camp. He was a mighty tired cowboy. His bedroll was a welcome sight.

Slim Jim Watkins stripped off all his duds, all but his long johns and his new britches. Then he collapsed into his bedroll. No sooner did he lay his head on his hat than he was sound asleep. "Snort-whew!"

"Rise and shine!" roared the chuck-wagon cook. Slim Jim Watkins stretched, yawned, and reached for his bandanna.

"My bandanna! It's gone." Slim Jim Watkins searched and searched, but could not find his bandanna. Finally, he went to work.

"Dern!" growled Slim Jim Watkins. He coughed and choked from the dirt riled up by the cattle. "I need my bandanna!"

That night, Slim Jim Watkins traded a week's worth of dish washing for the cook's bandanna. After doing dishes, Slim Jim Watkins was one tired cowboy.

He stumbled to his bedroll and stripped off his duds, all but his worn long johns, new britches, and new bandanna. That night, he was so tired, he forgot to lay his head on his hat.

Soon after, the chuck-wagon cook clanged his pots together and yelled, *"Rise and shine."*

Slim Jim Watkins stretched and . . . "My hat! Where's my hat?!"

Slim Jim Watkins jumped to his feet. Frantically, he searched.

"Losin' my britches and bandanna is one thing, but to lose my hat is something else again!"

"Get to work!" boomed the trail boss.
So Slim Jim Watkins went to work without his hat.
"Dern!" beefed Slim Jim Watkins when the blistering sun burnt his face. "I need my hat!"

So Slim Jim Watkins rode into town to buy a hat.

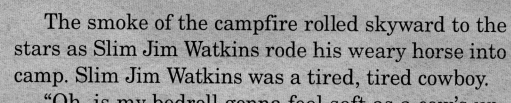

The smoke of the campfire rolled skyward to the stars as Slim Jim Watkins rode his weary horse into camp. Slim Jim Watkins was a tired, tired cowboy.

"Oh, is my bedroll gonna feel soft as a cow's underside tonight!"

Sitting beside his bedroll, Slim Jim Watkins started to pull off his boots.

"On second thought," he said, "I'm gonna sleep just the way I am." And he did, boots and all.

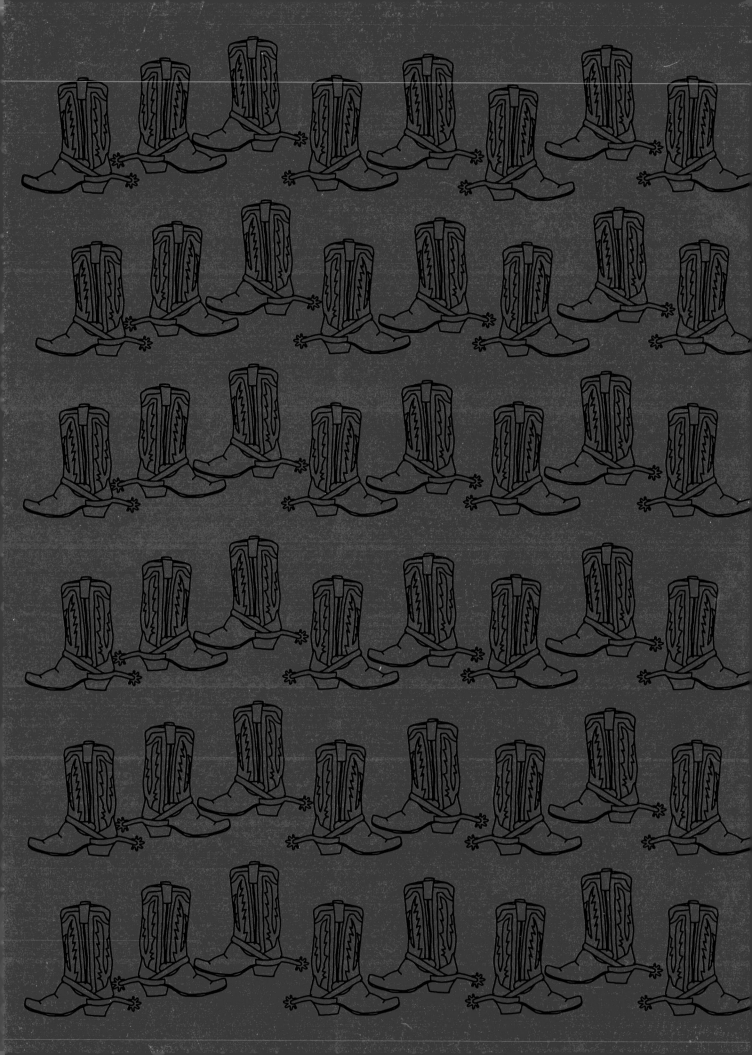